THE GREAT POSSUM CREEK DROUGHT

THIS BOOK BELONGS TO

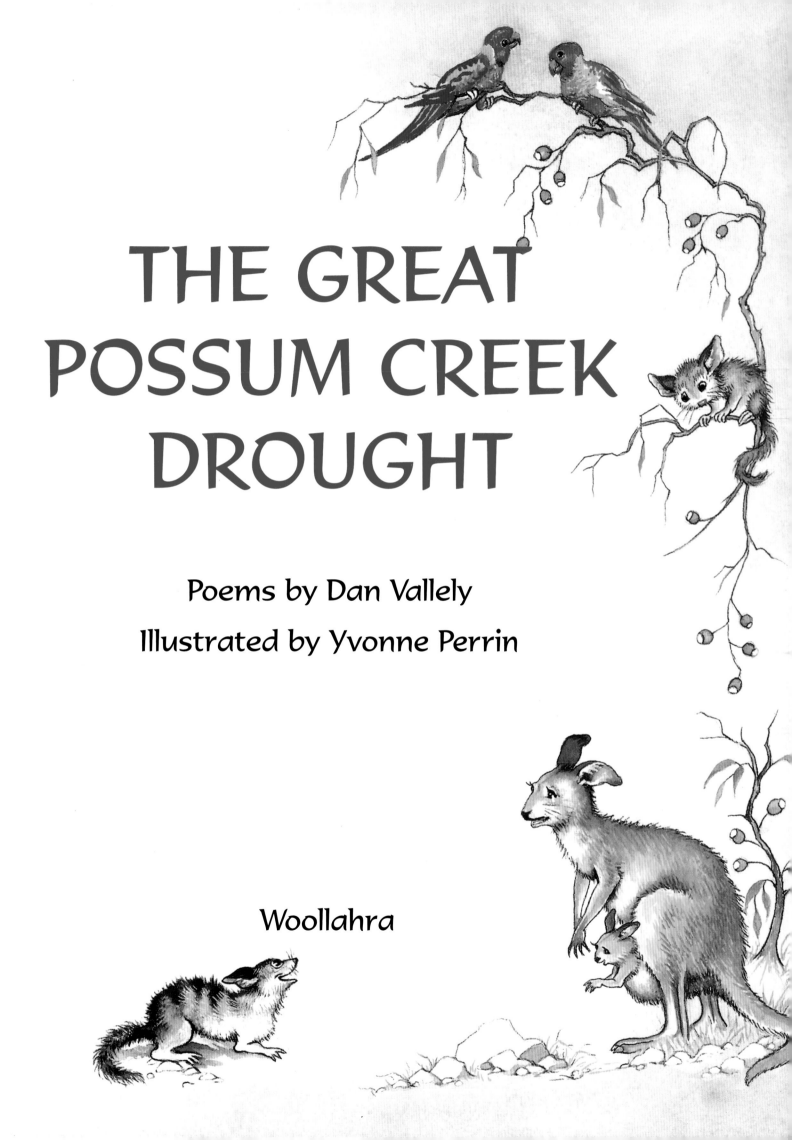

THE GREAT POSSUM CREEK DROUGHT

Poems by Dan Vallely

Illustrated by Yvonne Perrin

Woollahra

Wally Wombat gave a sigh
As he cast a troubled eye
On the rolling hills that once had been so green.
Months of unrelenting drought
Had transformed it, without doubt,
Into what was now a brown and dusty scene.

WONGI LAKE

Wongi Lake was almost dry,
They must find a new supply
Of fresh water or alas within a week,
Though the notion might appal,
Every creature large and small
Would be forced to leave the town of Possum Creek.

Big Red Kangaroo was stressed
And it's truthful to suggest
That his hop had been reduced to half or less.
Platypus was feeling grim,
There was nowhere left to swim
And poor Ed Galah was really just a mess!

'Twas Professor Cockatoo
Who, at length, expressed the view
That he'd have to find a way and find it quick.
"I'm afraid", he said, "it's plain
That it's not about to rain.
I'll design a new device to do the trick".

So he locked himself away
For a weekend and a day
And he thought and clanked and banged
And clanked and thought.
All the creatures crossed their paws,
It was such a vital cause,
And they hoped his efforts wouldn't come to nought.

Then one morning it was done,
And there shining in the sun
Stood the most peculiar, strangely shaped machine.
It had seven gleaming rows
Of steel teeth upon its nose
And it looked like a giant jelly bean!

The Professor, clearly proud,
Then addressed the gawking crowd
And he told them with a great amount of zeal,
"I propose dear friends to go
On a mission down below
In my Turbo Charged Terrific Digmobile!"

"There is water, cool and sweet,
Many metres 'neath our feet
And I'm sure I can locate it with your aid."
And with little more ado
Why his old familiar crew
Joined the scholar for his brand new escapade!

The Professor threw a switch,
With a tremble and a twitch
She jerked into life and bored into the ground.
There was nothing to be seen
Through the special toughened screen
As she ploughed on with a rumbling roaring sound.

Peter Possum sang a song
As they clanked and whirred along,
Everyone was brave for so much was at stake.
Through red clay and shale and rock,
With a shudder and a shock
They broke through into a great artesian lake.

They could not escape their fate,
The water pressure was so great
That it carried all before it, yes indeed.
There was nothing they could do,
Backwards up the shaft they flew
To the surface, at a quite amazing speed.

Through the air upon that spout
The Digmobile came shooting out.
The creatures trembled, but upon that lucky day
They missed houses, rocks and trees,
And crash landed if you please
Very softly in a mouldy stack of hay!

WONGI LAKE

Well, the water flowed so fast
That before a week had passed
Wongi Lake had reached its highest level yet.
And the good Professor's bore
Would ensure forever more,
That in future, droughts would never pose a threat!

The
End

Other titles in this series:

Possum One the Outback Rocketship
Possum Creek's Big Flood
The Great Possum Creek Bush Fire
Professor Cockatoo's Amazing Weatherdust
The Great Possum Creek Earthquake
The Lost World of Possum Creek
The Possum Creek Olympics

Also illustrated by Yvonne Perrin:

Australian Poems to read to the very young
Banjo Paterson's Animals Noah Forgot